PRAISE FOR

Tom Clancy fans open to a strong female lead will clamor for more.

— *Drone*, Publishers Weekly

Superb!

— *Drone*, Booklist starred review

The best military thriller I've read in a very long time. Love the female characters.

— *Drone,* Sheldon McArthur, founder of
The Mystery Bookstore, LA

A fabulous soaring thriller.

— *Take Over at Midnight,* Midwest Book
Review

Meticulously researched, hard-hitting, and suspenseful.

— *Pure Heat,* Publishers Weekly, starred
review

Expert technical details abound, as do realistic military missions with superb imagery that will have readers feeling as if they are right there in the midst and on the edges of their seats.

— *LIGHT UP THE NIGHT,* RT REVIEWS, 4 1/2 STARS

Buchman has catapulted his way to the top tier of my favorite authors.

— FRESH FICTION

Nonstop action that will keep readers on the edge of their seats.

— *TAKE OVER AT MIDNIGHT,* LIBRARY JOURNAL

M L. Buchman's ability to keep the reader right in the middle of the action is amazing.

— LONG AND SHORT REVIEWS

The only thing you'll ask yourself is, "When does the next one come out?"

— *WAIT UNTIL MIDNIGHT,* RT REVIEWS, 4 STARS

The first...of (a) stellar, long-running (military) romantic suspense series.

I knew the books would be good, but I didn't realize how good.

Buchman mixes adrenalin-spiking battles and brusque military jargon with a sensitive approach.

13 times "Top Pick of the Month"

LIFEBOAT LOVE

A US COAST GUARD ROMANTIC SUSPENSE STORY

M. L. BUCHMAN

Buchman Bookworks

SIGN UP FOR M. L. BUCHMAN'S NEWSLETTER TODAY

Other works by M. L. Buchman:

Contemporary Romance (cont)

Where Dreams
Where Dreams are Born
Where Dreams Reside
Where Dreams Are of Christmas
Where Dreams Unfold
Where Dreams Are Written

Science Fiction / Fantasy

Deities Anonymous
Cookbook from Hell: Reheated
Saviors 101

Single Titles
The Nara Reaction
Monk's Maze
the Me and Elsie Chronicles

Non-Fiction

Strategies for Success
Managing Your Inner Artist/Writer
Estate Planning for Authors*
Character Voice
Narrate and Record Your Own
Audiobook*

Short Story Series by M. L. Buchman:

Romantic Suspense

Delta Force
Delta Force

Firehawks
The Firehawks Lookouts
The Firehawks Hotshots
The Firebirds

The Night Stalkers
The Night Stalkers
The Night Stalkers 5E
The Night Stalkers CSAR
The Night Stalkers Wedding Stories

US Coast Guard
US Coast Guard

White House Protection Force
White House Protection Force

Contemporary Romance

Eagle Cove
Eagle Cove

Henderson's Ranch
Henderson's Ranch*

Where Dreams
Where Dreams

Thrillers

Dead Chef
Dead Chef

Science Fiction / Fantasy

Deities Anonymous
Deities Anonymous

Other
The Future Night Stalkers
Single Titles

ABOUT THIS BOOK

After failing to land themselves Coast Guard husbands, **local women Tabby and Suzy** *set off from Astoria, Oregon to find a future of their own making.*

Rescue Swimmer Tad *and his* **rescue-helo Crew Chief Craig** *have been playing the field together at the bars for years. But when the two women return to town as Coast Guard lifeboat drivers, all roaming thoughts are soon lost at sea—target acquired.*

1

"THERE'S SOMETHING WRONG WITH THESE PEOPLE," CRAIG waved his sandwich at the rest of the table.

"Says the dude eating a clubhouse like the pansy he is." Tad held up his own monstrous Buschman Burger, dripping with mushrooms, onions, and cheese out every side to make his point. The Workers Tavern was crowded with locals and off-duty Coasties, and most of them, Tad was glad to see, ate real food—not little triangular sandwiches on white toast.

The USCG Station Cape Disappointment and its Motor Lifeboat School were just over the big bridge in Ilwaco, Washington. And the rescue helos of USCG Sector Columbia River were planted at the Astoria, Oregon airport on this side. There were also a pair of two-hundred-and-ten-foot cutters perched at the Astoria docks when they weren't out saving people's asses.

Meeting in the middle at Workers, nestled under the big bridge that crossed the four-mile width of the mouth of the Columbia River was a thing long before he and Craig had shown up.

"Just shows I've got taste." Craig grimaced at Tad's burger. It was an argument that had gone back to their third day of deployment together four years ago and they'd joyfully never resolved it.

"Just shows you're a lazy crew chief, sitting on your ass in the helo, while us swimmers do the real work."

"Fine, next time I won't haul you back out of the ocean after a rescue and you may content yourself with swimming home."

Tad decided he was too hungry to keep it going, so he took a big bite of his burger before he remembered Craig's comment and looked around their table. "*Whuf* ifz rong mif deez people?" he managed.

Craig rolled his eyes, then waved at the two couples sharing their table.

The cutter *Steadfast* was in to dock so Hailey and Vera, the two Landing Safety Officers, were ashore. And they sat with their helo-pilot husbands. It wouldn't be quite so irksome if they weren't all happier'n roosters-in-the-henhouse about it. *And* it was just rotten luck that they were the two pilots for his and Craig's rescue helo.

Sly and Ham just never shut up about these two women. Which was nauseating...except it wasn't.

He'd liked Vera when they did a cave rescue together. Hot, funny, but with an elegance that looked amazing on her. And Hailey was a hell of a laugh. The four of them actually made it look as if happy-ever-after existed.

Tad scanned the dive bar.

It looked the same as always. Battered as a twenty-year-old manure spreader. The only reason it didn't collapse into the river and wash away was because it lay a block back from the waterfront. The late afternoon June sunlight sparkled off the sea salt that hadn't been washed off from March's final storm. The light was out there, it just didn't dare come inside which gave the place a muddy but comfortable feel.

Beer and booze signs on three walls; the fourth was covered in small bills from a hundred or more countries —for almost a hundred years mariners had been filling in the gaps on that wall of Workers Tavern.

The big U-shaped bar took up half the space. Four old graybeards, too aged to go out to sea, sat in their usual spot telling lies and singing off-key harmonies to the jukebox. The tiny kitchen in the back offered the best meat in town. And the scattering of tables looked just as work-worn as the graybeards.

But the bar looked different in some way.

Normally when he scanned it, he'd see if there were any likely women about. Charlene was in, but she already had some boy-o at her side. She was fun, but not enough to get upset about. There was a new pair of fairly hot chicks he hadn't seen before, but he'd spotted them holding hands when they came in, and were now very cozy at the bar. Nothing happening there.

Tonight though, it all looked just a little *too* familiar. All the training time and hard work, yet all he'd done was trade one small town for another. Not a chance was he going to find what the Coasties sitting at his table seemed to have in spades. Of course, they hadn't fallen for local talent: these Coasties had married Coasties. Local talent was *always* a bad bet.

Didn't matter. He'd never wanted that cute-couple stamp anyway.

But...they did make it *look* damn tasty.

Maybe he'd better stick with harassing Craig and eating his Buschman Burger. At least those he understood.

2

"YOU READY FOR THIS?" SUZY GRIPPED THE RUSTED DOOR handle of Workers Tavern.

"So not. It looks even worse than the last time we were here. What delusion makes you think I want to do this?" Tabby Alton would rather throw herself off the pier. Of course, it was June, so it wouldn't be that much of a hardship—until the Columbia's fierce current swept her out to sea.

"You remember what Marj Kaye used to say."

Tabby sighed. No need to make it a question because of course she did.

They spoke in unison. "You've got to face your *shit* and move on." Their third-grade teacher never would have deigned to say "shit" of course, but all of the kids had picked it up that way as soon as Suzy had modified it.

"But why?" Tabby waved a hand at the tavern. It was a dark hole under the on-ramp to the soaring Astoria-Megler suspension bridge. A place filled with memories of who they *used* to be. How many nights had they come

here in tight tank tops to troll for a USCG husband? Way
too many.

"Because," Suzy swung open the door. Seared meat,
spilled beer, and off-key music reeled drunkenly out onto
the sidewalk, stumbling on the cracks. "I'm hoping that
Vivian is here. I'd like to thank her."

"Oh, okay." That was good. She'd thought it might be
one of her best friend's long-running guy quests that she
was inevitably swept up in.

A year ago they'd been majorly chatting up a pair of
Coastie officers right here in Workers—best chance at
getting out that an Astoria girl could have. Then a female
petty officer had nudged her way onto *their* table, busting
up the play but good. The guys left. PO Vivian Schroder
had delivered a lecture on all that it took to escape a town
was *leaving.* And that until they'd looked around the
outside world for themselves, they'd never know what
they really wanted, or deserved.

Vivian had been hella persuasive. She made it all
sound so real and possible. So they'd gone. Bus to
Portland, then Suzy's whim had led them south. They'd
ended up frying donuts in a hole in Alameda called Lee's.
It wasn't really a hole; it was just another place in another
strip mall in an upscale neighborhood close to the water
—though a step down from the Blue Scorcher back home
—the best bakery in Astoria.

She'd been the one who'd walked into the Coast
Guard Recruiting office on the other side of the building
from Lee's. Maybe it had been a fit of nostalgia for
Astoria. Or maybe just wanting to see an eligible male
not stuffing his waistline with lemon-filled carbs soaked

in sugar, then glazed, then topped with sprinkles. Even the sight of a sprinkle had made her nauseous since then. Neither one of them ended up dating the recruiter, but they'd walked out of the office signed up to serve.

Weirdly, training had suited both of them down to their boots. When it came time to file a Station preference, it had barely taken a glance at each other before they both wrote Astoria in the blank.

Steppenwolf's *Magic Carpet Ride* wandered out the door and thankfully faded fast into sunset—gone before the second verse.

"I wonder if Sly and Ham are still here?" Suzy remarked before breezing through the door to Workers Tavern.

"I *knew* it!" But Tabby was standing outside talking to herself. She hadn't even remembered their names, but Suzy never forgot a guy. She was like a flirt-savant.

Resigned to her doom, Tabby stepped out of the bright light of the long evening into near darkness of the tavern. She ran into Suzy's back and almost knocked her to the floor.

"What?"

"They *are* here."

"Where?" She followed the angle of Suzy's head; ever since kindergarten it was the very best indicator of where the cute guys were.

She recognized them easily. Ham dark as night and Sly looking like he'd last sunbathed, maybe, in a former life. She'd remembered them as so dashing and so much larger than life.

They still were pretty dashing, but they appeared to

be more human-sized. She and Suzy were Coast
Guardswomen now, so it brought the two officers into
somewhat sharper focus. Sure they were just E-3 grade
Seaman, but E-4 Petty Officer Third Class was looming
near, if they did well on their first real assignment.

But Sly and Ham were already sitting next to two
women, also clearly in the Guard. There was just
something about how a trained sailor sat that said they
weren't locals.

She also noticed the two other men at the table. The
one with his back to her had the unmistakable shoulders
of a rescue swimmer, and he wasn't Harvey.

"Vivian's gone." A different swimmer and crew chief
now sat to Ham's and Sly's other side from the women.

"Aw shit. Maybe they'll know where she went." And
Suzy just walked right up to the table. Nothing about
socially awkward, or time to turn tail and run. They'd
both been more than willing to bed the two pilots on the
off chance of getting a ring from them. And they'd all
four known those terms.

She spotted the sparkler on each of the women's
hands. Yep! Married. The two Guardswomen had pulled
off what she and Suzy hadn't been able to—even if she
and Suzy had been doing it for all the wrong reasons.

"Hey Sly. Hi Ham." Suzy planted herself at the end of
the table by the two new guys. "Is Vivian still around?"

Sly looked over and called out cheerily, "Hey Suzy!
Long time no see." Because he was just as unflappable as
Suzy.

Ham looked up, first at Suzy, then at her. It took him a
moment, then he blinked hard. His expression clearly

said that if his skin had been lighter it would be shining red with a blush.

"Naw! She and Harvey shipped out to Hawaii for their honeymoon and never came back."

Tabby could feel the blood drain from her face.

Ham spoke softly. "Not dead. They signed up over there. Warm water rescuer."

"Yeah, left the cold shit to me." The swimmer, who still had his back to her, said with deep chagrin and a bit of humor.

3

TAD COULD FEEL SOMETHING. THE SWIMMER'S ITCH. At sea, a swimmer never knew what they'd encounter during a rescue and had to develop "ten-eighty" awareness.

The best swimmer he'd ever met, Senior Chief Vernon, had insisted that knowing three-sixty degrees around you in water wasn't enough. A collapsing mast could come from above, the lash of a snapping line from behind, a shark from below, and a wave from any damn direction it was in the mood for.

"Three-sixty around, three-sixty over, and three-sixty under. One-thousand-and-eighty-degree awareness at all times. Forget about a single slice of that ten-eighty and it *will* get you. You know what happens then?"

"You die, Senior Chief," had been his naive answer.

"No, you idiot. The people depending on you to rescue them die. That's a thousand times worse. Got it, Meat?" He'd called all swimmer hopefuls that. Just meat for the grinder that was swimmer school and its eighty percent failure rate.

"Yes, Senior Chief."

Then ten minutes later Vernon would prove that Tad didn't have a clue, again.

The proudest day of his life hadn't been making it to rescue swimmer. It had been the Senior Chief shaking his hand after graduation. "Go make us proud, Swimmer."

Tad knew no higher praise.

And right now, his swimmer's itch—another of Vernon's phrases—was itching something fierce.

Sparky brunette beside him. Excellent breasts under a Coastie-blue tee, right at eye-level as he was sitting, so he let himself enjoy the view for a moment before looking farther afield. Face was no disappointment. You could just tell she had a sass-factor set to permanent high. Even so, rigidly posted in an "at ease" stance, she stood like a first-year addressing officers on base. It always took them a while to chill in public.

At the bar, the old guys were swaying their way through the Beatles' *When I'm Sixty-four,* an age they'd abandoned decades before. That the Stones were rocking *Wild Horses* on the juke didn't seem to faze them. Grandma had always been a hardcore Beatles' fan. *None of those upstart Stones in my house.* Because he landed on her side of the duplex every day after school, he knew all thirteen core albums by heart. Grandma wasn't one for remixes and US re-releases.

Sly was grinning up at the lady attached to the nice breasts. The two of them were tossing it back and forth like it was old times. At least until Hailey fisted him pretty hard in the ribs.

Vera had no need to tap Ham; he was looking thoroughly embarrassed. Had they both dallied with Ms. Breasts and now...

No, Ham wasn't looking at the sparky brunette but rather behind Tad's back.

He glanced around.

Then he fully turned to get a better view.

Cut from the same cloth, yet totally different. The quiet blonde was a study. Built just like her brunette pal, the same five-eight and fit-as-hell. Maybe a little more in the shoulder. But his gaze didn't even hesitate at her chest despite the same tight blue t-shirt. Her face and piercing blue eyes were far too arresting to waste time looking anywhere else.

"Ma'am," he greeted her respectfully enough to earn him a surprised laugh from Craig. The blonde was the sort to command respect.

She arched a single eyebrow.

"Grandma had that down." He touched his own forehead and pulled up his right eyebrow. "Scary as shit lady, I can tell you."

"And you loved her very much," the blonde said softly.

Tad didn't know that it was so obvious, but he shrugged its truth.

"Mine too. Grannie is awesome. And I was terrified of her every time I screwed up. Still am, I suppose."

Tad could just imagine Ms. Blonde being a scary grandma herself someday. Real easy to imagine.

4

"STILL SORRY WE CAME HOME?"

"Wrong time to ask." Tabby stared at the bilge of the forty-seven-foot Motor Lifeboat, 47-MLB, that they'd just spent two hours contorting themselves worse than a yoga class to scrub down. The bilge, the very bottom of the boat, sparkled. And every bit of grime, grease, and she didn't want to know what, was now embedded in her skin.

"I'm talking about the boys."

"You always are." Last night at Workers, everyone had squeezed over and they'd found one spare chair. She and Suzy had shared it, one cheek each. Suzy had spent the whole evening prodding at Craig's cultured Long Island, New York bonhomie. She and Tad had discussed grandmothers. His passed away three years back, hers still tenacious as could be, living alone out on the sandy, windswept side of Warrenton, Oregon. *House I was married in. House I'll die in.*

Tad had laughed. "Adair, Iowa. Not the sort of place

folks leave much. Excepting anyone who can figure a way out."

"Astoria, Oregon. Place I thought I'd never want to come back to."

She'd liked his easy laughter at himself. And despite all of his teasing of Craig, it was clear that he trusted him as only a rescue swimmer could trust his helo crew chief. Tad's life often truly depended on Craig just as much as others' lives depended on Tad going in the water.

But she and Suzy were assigned to the motor lifeboats on the other side of the Columbia River from the airport. They'd both chosen boat operations and there was no better berth they could have drawn. The Motor Lifeboat School, located at the Cape Disappointment Station— Cape D—on the Columbia River was the most prestigious school of its type in the world.

Suzy had taken her dad's penchant for being the town's best car mechanic straight into the engine room. Her own target, Boatswain's Mate, was going to be a long road before she could con her own boat. Senior Chief McAllister had made that clear when he'd assigned her to Sarah Goodwin's boat. And BM First Class, BM1, Sarah Goodwin had assigned her to help Suzy clean the bilge.

"A BM knows every inch of her boat and every skill of her crew."

Then she'd turned away as if neither of them existed. Now they crouched exhausted to either side of the immaculate twin Detroit diesel engines.

A voice came through the access hatch above. "You sure you know which side of the scrub brush cleans things up? Boat looks fine. But damn, girl."

Tabby looked up to see BM1 Sarah Goodwin smiling down at her.

Then the smile clicked off. "Five more just like her along the dock. Don't take so long this time."

Tabby stared down at the fouled water in her pail and considered throwing herself into it. Ugly way to drown, but still...six?

By the time they finished the other five boats, even Suzy wasn't wasting energy talking about guys.

5

TAD TRIED TO THINK OF HOW TO BRING IT UP WITHOUT quite bringing it up. "Haven't seen much of the girls lately." Okay, subtle was never his best play. *Subtle as a bull in heat,* Paw had always said of him all the way back to T-ball days. Tad had ruled first base, *the* hot spot in T-ball.

"Suzy is a pain in the behind," though Craig didn't sound very put out by it. He held out a hand for the wrench he'd asked Tad to hold. He was up on a ladder with his head inside the engine cowling of their HH-65 Dolphin rescue helo checking that all of the fittings were tight.

Tad ignored the waving hand and practiced twirling the wrench back and forth through his fingers. It was a move he could do in his sleep.

Craig extracted himself enough from the open cowling to look down at Tad from the top of the step ladder. "Uh-oh! I know that look."

"What look?"

"The one while you're thinking. You're a swimmer, Tad, just give it up and accept that your brain isn't your best asset."

Tad twirled the wrench a few more times just out of Craig's reach to prove that he had skills. He mis-timed Craig's reach and accidentally smacked his knuckles rather than slapping it into his crew chief's palm.

"Ow! Crap! Well, at least that proves my point."

"What point?" A voice asked from behind him.

Tad swung around to stare at Tabby standing right in his six. And he hadn't even felt her there. She was absolutely screwing with his situational awareness. Her golden hair was all stirred up. He could hear the wind that had done it, slamming against the hangar, and told himself *not* to reach out to smooth it back into place though his fingers ached to do so.

"Helo engine? Cool!" And Suzy scrambled up the back side of Craig's ladder until she was standing chest to chest with him, but all of her attention was on the engine. Or at least she was making Craig think so.

True to form, Craig fell for it and didn't notice the lush female practically pressed against him. Instead, he began walking her through the engine.

Tad wasn't quite so dense, and turned back to Tabby. "Where've you been hiding?" Still had apparently left all his smooth back in Iowa.

"I've been wondering something. How does a US Coast Guard swimmer end up coming from Iowa?" Tabby answered his question with a question.

"Lifeguard at the beach some."

"They have beaches in Iowa?"

"Aw, sure. Mine musta been most of a hundred feet long. Swimming hole dug out of the field by Old Man Jasper just off 1st Street."

"So, major surf wasn't a big deal." Damn but the woman had a great smile, slow and trending just a little sideways. Craig and Suzy had sealed up the engine cowling and were now inside the helo going over who cared about what.

"If you don't count when Fat Steve did cannonballs off the diving board, not so much. But I mighta also spent some summers with my uncle, a Coronado Beach SEAL. He had this thing about swimming skills." He was the one who'd taught Tad how to dream bigger than a haystack or a wheat field. It had set his future path forever apart from his Adair classmates and Tad blessed him every day for that.

That pulled out Tabby's rare laugh. Suzy was always on the edge of one, bursting forth at the least provocation —even now sounding from behind him. Tabby's was shy as a newborn barn cat, always lurking half out of sight.

"Where did you get *your* taste for water?"

"Local, remember?"

He smacked his forehead. Born and raised along the Columbia, looking out at some of the most beautiful and absolutely the most dangerous water in the world.

"Okay, local. So, where you been, local lady? Checking out old high school boyfriends?" *Please say no.* She was here at the airport, wasn't she?

"Oh sure. All of the most eligible guys in the world were born and raised right here in Astoria. You know all the ones who don't work the boats work the fryer at

McDonald's, right? So we've been hanging at McD's big time. Nothing else to do in this town." Her final grimace spoke volumes. He'd bet that she and Suzy had spent many high school afternoons doing just that.

"Wouldn't know about that. Adair was too small for a Macs. We've got Zipp's Pizza and the Chuckwagon. Oh, I think they've got a Subway now. *All* the hot babes in Iowa work at Subway, you know."

"Maybe we should introduce them. All your farmer girls and all our lame-o non-fisher boys."

"Deal," he reached out and she shook on it. Despite sitting knee-to-knee several times at Workers, it was the first time they'd actually touched. Her hand felt small and feminine in his, despite its strength. Rather than letting go, he turned it and looked down. "Someone's been fighting the grime." Embedded dark around the joints, and under chipped nails; good calluses, too. About the nicest hands he'd ever met.

"You've never seen six motor lifeboats as clean and shiny as the six at Cape D."

"They working you too hard?" He teased her a bit.

"Got this Boatswain's Mate thinks I should know every bolt of the boat and is shocked that I don't."

"Right, 'cause you've been here like seven whole days. He sounds like a hard ass."

"She, and you have no idea. I want to be just like her when I grow up."

No question who she was talking about. Sarah Goodwin's reputation was totally solid. "Not gonna find a better instructor than Sarah anywhere in the Coast Guard."

"If I survive it." But Tabby's smile as she recovered her hand said she was totally down with the challenge.

He'd never been much of hand holder, but he could feel the memory of her fingers curled up in his palm like a fresh-hatched chick.

6

TABBY'S PHONE RANG LOUD; MADE HER JUMP. SHE DIDN'T like letting anything show when she was surprised, but her mind had drifted as Tad held her hand. The raw power of the man was amazing. She could feel every bit of his immense strength—yet his control as well. He'd held her hand like he'd never let go, but not with some overtight grip.

"Hi. This is Tabby."

There was a brief pause. "This live Tabby, or recording Tabby?" BM1 Sarah Goodwin asked sharply.

"Live version." She really had to change how she answered the phone. She got that question all the time.

"Good. Where are you two?"

"Coast Guard helo hangar in Astoria."

"God damn it all to hell!" The vitriol was lethal.

"We were cleared off base, Bosun." Tabby replied carefully, hopefully a fair defense.

"I'm down a crew member and we've got an imminent rescue. Figured between you two that you could cover for him. How fast can you get here? Shit. Never mind. Forty minutes. I'm screwed and stuck at the dock."

Ten miles line-of-sight was a slow twenty-mile drive through town and then over the tall Astoria-Megler Bridge.

Even as Sarah fumed, the two pilots came rushing in. Maybe they'd gotten the rescue call as well.

Tabby had an idea. Just maybe... "Hold on, Sarah."

"For what?"

Tabby didn't answer, instead she listened.

"How fast can we get aloft?" Sly called out.

She liked that Tad and Craig barely had to exchange a glance before they answered in unison, "Three minutes."

"Do it! Your bird, Ham, get us spinning."

Tad had already stripped off his shirt as he headed to the equipment rack at the side of the hangar. Moments later he was down to tighty-whities. She knew that rescue swimmers were among the most fit of anyone in any service, but seeing it spelled out in rippling muscle across his back, butt, and legs was...

Her mind blanked.

"I know that look," Sly spoke up close beside her. "Hell, if I weren't straight and married, I'd be all over that." He bumped his shoulder against hers, then turned for his helo.

"Captain...Uh..." Tabby couldn't remember his last name. Suzy would know, of course, but she was busy watching Hammond doing the engine startup procedure.

"Captain Uh, that's me." Sly stopped and smiled at her.

"Sorry about that, sir. This is a bit presumptuous."

"Better ask quick, we're on the bounce." But he wasn't brushing her off.

"Our Bosun, Petty Officer Goodwin, is down a crew member. I'm guessing she got the same call you did. She's asked how fast we could get there."

"That her?" Sly pointed toward the phone that Tabby had completely forgotten she was holding.

Sly slipped it out of her fingers. "Sarah? Sly here. We're aloft in two; you'll have your crew in five. You owe me." He handed back the phone without waiting for an answer and waved her toward the helo's cargo bay with a grin.

"We're on our way, Sarah," she said into the phone even as she waved Suzy aboard.

"So I heard. Done good. Keep surprising me, *Seaman*." She hit last word hard to remind Tabby not to be too uppity in using her given name, then PO Goodwin was gone.

Tabby climbed aboard mere seconds ahead of Tad in full swimmer's gear. He now wore form-hugging International Orange neoprene, with an inflatable life vest and a small utility belt. Fins and a snorkel stuck out of a gear bag as he tugged on his helmet.

The transformation was magical. In such simple gear, he was now headed out to jump into the rough waters of the Pacific Ocean to save other people's lives. He looked...amazing!

"How far you going with us, Tabby?" He asked happily as he settled in his seat against the rear bulkhead.

"Just as far as Cape D."

Suzy grinned and rolled her eyes at her.

"Oh." Somewhere along the way she'd become the perfect fall girl for a straight line. But she hadn't been best friends with Suzy for over eighteen years and learned nothing. "Depends on how far *you* want to go, Swimmer." It wasn't the smoothest recovery, but it worked. Also, once she said it, it felt surprisingly true.

He burst out laughing as the helo lifted and Craig slammed the side doors shut. "Stick with the straight lines, pretty lady. They fit you way better."

Okay, hopefully her crew skills would be better than her so-not-Suzy flirt skills.

7

Tad saw the change come over her. Something shifted after he hit her with that off-hand tease.

She sat straighter. Gave a half nod to herself as she tugged her t-shirt smooth. She'd tried to flirt a little, and it hadn't fit her at all. Just not the person she was. Not that she was bad at it; she'd delivered the line perfectly and definitely sent his imagination to some very nice places.

But it didn't fit his *image* of her.

And if he was reading her face right—he'd become a good judge of expressions in all of his rescues—it abruptly didn't fit her own image of herself either. Not even a little.

He glanced at Suzy. She was looking at Tabby, they were sitting almost knee-to-knee on the cargo bay deck, but she wasn't seeing it. Suzy should be the one he was attracted to. Flirty and funny. Smart, but not real interested in deeper thought.

No question but Tabby was a deep thinker. And it

looked as if she just pulled it on like a skin tighter than his wetsuit.

Ham barely hesitated as the girls dumped out at Cape D. Back in the air, Tad watched them sprinting down the dock toward one of the boats.

He also noticed that Craig had slid his own seat, mounted on a side-to-side rail at the front of the cabin, so that he too could watch them run.

"What do ya think, buddy boy?"

Craig shook his head bemused. "Swears she never looked at a turboshaft engine before, but she just…got it. Somewhere inside that lovely woman is a very sharp mechanic."

Tad snorted. "That's you all over. A crew chief first and a man ninety-third. Bet you didn't even notice her pressing her chest against you up on that ladder."

Craig grinned at him. "I noticed plenty. A ladder is just a little precarious for what ideas she brought to mind. Noticed you were actually holding Tabby's hand without dragging her off to the nearest closet."

"Maybe," he shrugged. It didn't sound like him.

Then Sly came on the intercom. "If you two love birds can get some focus, we have a ship collision about ten miles northwest."

They spent the next couple minutes, as the helo raced out to sea, going over what little information was available. A fishing trawler and a coastal container ship had rammed one another in the wide-open ocean.

Neither was expected to stay afloat long.

The thick fog that always lay offshore had enveloped the wreck. It delayed them finding it for five painfully long minutes before they arrived above the tangled mess.

Tad had jumped crabbing boats off Alaska and sailboats caught in a nor'easter, but never in such weird weather. Clear blue skies above and out to the horizon. The tall Cascade Range stood out sharply against the summer sky. Below? Blowing thirty knots in a dense fog layer lumping over twenty-foot swells.

Looking off to either side, the sea was invisible past a few hundred meters.

Straight down, it was a disaster.

A typical fishing trawler might have merely damaged the container ship as it was sliced in two. No such luck, the cargo ship had rammed a fifty-meter stern trawler right up the kazoo. Rather than the bow just cutting the trawler in two, the trawler had been stout enough to sheer much of the bow off the container ship before it succumbed. The trawler was in two halves, with one of the halves already missing, probably at the bottom of the sea. And the container ship was nose-down with the foredeck awash.

Dozens of forty-foot steel shipping containers— maybe hundreds hiding within the fog—were floating about the two wrecked ships. The swells banged them together creating a floating hazard like none he'd ever seen.

"Where the hell do we begin?" Ham called over the radio.

Tad studied it for longer than his usual ten or so seconds. Long enough for Craig to make a worried sound.

The plan of attack was up to the rescue swimmer.

"How long to the next helo arriving?"

"Fifteen minutes," Sly reported. "About the same as the first MLBs."

There were rafts floating among the containers, bright orange dots. Here and there were tiny specks of crewmen in the water. They all were at risk from the debris.

Even as he watched, a pair of containers were thrown together so hard that he could hear the metal bang and crumple right over the sound of the Dolphin helo's twin turboshaft engines and pounding rotor.

And there were personnel still aboard both ships waving at his bird.

The Dolphin could pick up seven.

There were over thirty.

"The trawler hull is heading down first. Let's start there."

He could feel the desperation of the other seamen as the helo shifted toward the remaining half of the fishing trawler. Not everyone was coming home from this one.

Senior Chief Vernon had been clear on that. *Don't think. Act! You save every single one you can. Each one you save is one less for the sea.*

The lashing wires and tangled nets of the trawler meant they couldn't risk winching him down to the deck.

Craig called the position to Ham.

After they'd run the pre-swimmer-insertion checklist, all Tad focused on now was even-breathing and the security of his gear.

When Craig's slap landed on his shoulder, he launched feet first into the angry wreckage.

8

"OH. MY. GOD."

"I don't think God is helping much on this one," Sarah answered.

She and Tabby were standing side-by-side on the flying bridge of the 47-MLB. Suzy was down below checking on the engines. The boat's two rescue crew were down in the survivors' cabin—a six-seat watertight compartment directly below their feet. They were fully dressed in wetsuits and probably playing their usual gin rummy despite the rough ride.

Sarah may have been last off the line by eight minutes, but she'd sliced such a line through the surf over the Columbia River Bar that in the half an hour from Cape D, she was the lead boat.

"Wreckage at ten o'clock!" Tabby shouted and pointed off the left bow.

"Good eye," Sarah backed both engines hard. A container floated just awash, visible only as an incongruous flat spot in the wind-ripped water. "Swimmers ready?"

How was she supposed to know that?

Sarah had given them only minimal instructions as they'd raced aboard and yanked on their Mustang onsie float gear.

The orientation for their first real-world rescue had been brief and to the point. "Engineer got some bad fish and is blowing at both ends with food poisoning. Between you two, you're covering. Suzy, just keep my boat running. Tabby, you're my right hand. Don't even think of doing something without clearing it with me. Either of you ever unhook both of your safety lines at the same time, I'm gonna leave you behind after you're washed overboard." End of conversation.

So, Tabby got ready to go find out if the swimmers were ready. They weren't rescue swimmers like Tad—technically he was an Aviation Survival Technician. The only way the MLB's swimmers were allowed off the boat was if they were tied to the MLB on a line. But they were still incredible swimmers.

She turned and would have fallen over backwards if she hadn't been harnessed into her seat—they were both standing close behind her.

"They're ready," she reported.

Sarah may have smiled; she couldn't have missed Tabby's flinch.

"Let's start with the rafts before one of them gets pancaked," Sarah shouted over the grinding scrape of a container thrown out of a wave hard enough to peel open the container they'd almost hit. It sank before she could get a look at the contents.

Tabby held her breath as a sheet of spray plowed across the bridge. Once she'd wiped her eyes, she could see two rafts. The first was closer, and the other was being batted about a floating container. She automatically pointed to the second.

"I like your instinct," Sarah shouted over the roar of the boat's engines as she fought clear of another wave. "You do remember to think safety first, right?"

"Isn't it supposed to be, 'That Others May Live'?"

"That's the swimmer's creed, not the Coast Guards'. Of course," Sarah aimed for the imperiled raft. "I've always liked that creed." Her grin was wicked as she intentionally rammed the nose of the MLB into the container, then laid in full power to shove it clear of the raft.

The boat's swimmers were back on the aft deck. She spotted them coming up on her side of the boat where the side walkway dropped within a foot of the water to aid rescues just like this.

"Swimmers on the port side," she shouted to Sarah.

"Good. Call the distances."

And she did, as they slid nearer and nearer the raft. Three faces peered out the opening in the protective canopy. Once close enough, one of the swimmers snapped a line onto the raft as the other began hauling people out of it. Two men and one woman were directed to the afterdeck. Only one man was in Mustang float gear. The woman wore standard slicks, and the last guy had little more than jeans and a jacket. He was in bad shape and had to be carried up the three steps from the rescue well.

After they double-checked the raft, the swimmers slashed its inflated sides, and released it. It sunk out of sight in moments.

"Why not recover it?" Tabby shouted as Sarah carved a hard turn for the second raft.

"You'll see."

Tabby had some theories about—

The bow of the fishing trawler shot out the front of the wave and nearly skewered them. A 47' Motor Lifeboat, not matter how tough, was no match for a hundred-and-sixty-foot section of fishing trawler.

Two helos and their swimmers were working the other side of the wreckage. Two more MLBs had arrived while they were rescuing the first raft's crew. She barely had time to hope that Tad was being safe.

They spent ten minutes dodging around, trying to reach the other raft. It was a standard eight-person octagonal with a full canopy. After each successive wave, Tabby could find no way to predict its next position.

Finally, another MLB managed to catch it.

Tabby watched as they snapped on a line, looked inside, then slashed and sank it.

"We both just spent ten minutes chasing a raft that no one had gotten into. Knew it was light by the way it skittered around, but we had to check. Could have been a kid aboard. Now we slash it so that no one else wastes any more time on it."

Tabby nodded, searched around for the next raft, and then spotted Tad.

He had emerged from the face of a wave dragging a person not twenty feet from her boat.

"Swimmer in the water!" she shouted.

Sarah slowed, backed, and lined her boat up as the wave lifted behind them.

Tabby could feel the punch through her feet as the wave picked up Tad and his rescue and slammed them into the side of the boat just below her feet.

Hopefully the loud clang was the hard slap of the wave and not Tad's head against the hull.

9

"GRAB HIM!" TAD SHOUTED WITH WHAT LITTLE AIR WAS left in his body after the hard hit.

Two hands reached down from above and grabbed the collar of the guy. Tad wasn't sure if the guy was still alive, but he'd gotten him out of the maelstrom.

His helo had been fully loaded so he'd waved them ashore. Since then he'd been swimming from body to body until he found a live one. Then he set out with everything he had left to reach the MLB he'd spotted playing a game of dodgeball with a cluster of containers.

Ten minutes of hard swimming he was nearly played out.

On the next wave, the guy he'd rescued was floated right out of his hands and up onto the flying bridge.

In moments, the guy was strapped into the spare seat behind the two pilot positions.

Then the assistant bosun looked back over the rail at him.

His ears were still ringing with his impact against the

boat. The roar of wave and engine drowned out all other sound.

But there was no mistaking the worried words forming on Tabby's lips, "You okay?"

He checked. Nothing broken despite a few spots dancing in front of his eyes.

Tad pointed two fingers to his own eyes, then at her, then out at the water. Her extra six feet of elevation would give her a better view. Cold, tired, and ringing ears weren't going to be slowing him down.

And like the warrior she was, she didn't waste a moment. Instead, she went looking. When she shot an arm out to the rear, he dove back into the water and dug hard.

For the next hour, he followed the directions of his guiding angel, seeking survivors to haul back to her boat.

10

Tabby didn't know what to say to him.

They sat at the Workers Tavern bar, just next to the four graybeards, apparently on a musical siesta as they talked about sinkings of the past—some of which must have happened before even they were born.

Twice she'd seen a survivor, but in a position so dangerous that she didn't want to point him out to Tad. But, even knowing he'd go into the nightmare and perhaps not return, she gave him the signal—and he went.

The MLB's two swimmers often jumped in and swam out to the limits of their safety lines, to save Tad having to come all the way back to the boat.

And each time, he'd look to her as he tread water for a moment, and she'd find him another target.

"Nine," he whispered softly to his beer.

"No, twenty-four. We saved twenty-four."

"Nine didn't make it."

"No," she knew where he got the line. In the movie *The Guardian,* Kevin Costner played a rescue swimmer who only ever counted the lives he *hadn't* saved. It was probably the most aired movie in any Coast Guard Station.

Tad didn't look up at her.

She nudged him hard enough to make him turn to her.

"No, Tad. It doesn't work like that."

"Yeah, it does, sister."

"First, not your sister. Second, you were magnificent today. Did you save all those people because you said, 'I can't let one die.' Or did you do it because you said, 'I can save at least one more.' Go on, tell me it was the first one."

He blinked at her in surprise.

"You were..." the words caught in her throat but she didn't have any others, "...magnificent."

"I'm just a kid from Iowa."

"Who gives everything he's got to save one more person. Why are you in the Guard, Tad? I looked up your hometown. Adair is two hundred miles to the Mississippi and three hundred to Lake Michigan. How does a kid like that end up in the ocean off Astoria, Oregon?"

"How about you?" He fired it back like an accusation. "Shit! Sorry. Local girl. How many did you lose to the sea?"

"None. I've been lucky. Just turns out the sea is in my blood, even if I didn't know it."

Tad turned back to studying his half-empty beer.

Tabby didn't know how to reach him. Tad had

performed magic. Of the twenty-four saves, fifteen had been Tad's, despite two other boats and another helo's rescue swimmer being on site. And all he could see was the lives he *hadn't* saved.

"Girlie," one of the graybeards whispered to her. The other three were still reliving old wrecks.

"Yeah?"

"Ask him who he lost."

She could only blink at him in surprise.

His expression was sad with knowledge.

And then she knew. She squeezed the guy's gnarled hand in thanks and turned back to Tad.

"You loved your uncle very much, didn't you?"

In answer, Tad slowly twisted his beer back and forth between those strong hands that had saved so many lives.

Tabby rested her hand on his to quiet them.

He finally nodded. "Yeah. He died on a mission, shot down in Afghanistan. A SEAL, in the middle of the goddamn desert, his helo downed by an RPG. Never even had a goddamn chance to fight back. Should never have left the sea. He understood its ways like no man I've ever met. I save people because he died."

"No, Tad. You save people because of how he lived. He taught a little boy to love the sea."

Tad's hand finally went quiet under hers, as if he was frozen in place. Just as shocked as she'd been when Tad had pointed out that she wasn't some flirty chick like Suzy, who was being very cozy with Craig just now at one of the tables. No, Tabby had always survived by thinking hard and working hard—once she'd found her direction.

And Tad had given that to her in the hangar just this morning.

Then he slowly returned to twirling his beer, but didn't look up at her.

She almost turned back to the graybeard to see if he had any other advice, when Tad finally spoke again.

"Craig is always saying that I'm not smart enough to be anything other than a rescue swimmer. But I'm smart enough to figure out one thing."

"What's that?"

He turned to face her and took her hand between both of his. He squeezed it tightly while he closed his eyes for a long moment. When he opened them, he looked right at her.

"What?" She could feel the pounding in her ears as her heart tried to tell her something.

"No matter what Craig says, I'm smart enough to never, ever let you out of my life, Tabby."

"But..." Tabby didn't know what to say. "We've never even kissed."

"Remember what Craig said."

She had to laugh, "Not smart enough to be anything other than the most awesome rescue swimmer ever."

"Exactly. But I'm a quick learner." And he leaned in to kiss her.

She hesitated just long enough to identify the song the graybeards started singing.

Beatle's *Yellow Submarine?*

She couldn't help giggling into Tad's kiss. No question but they were going to be stuck with *that* as their song for the rest of their lives.

———

*If you enjoyed this, keep reading for an excerpt from a book
you're going to love.
..and a review is always welcome (it really helps)...*

OFF THE LEASH

IF YOU ENJOYED THIS, YOU'LL LOVE THE
WHITE HOUSE PROTECTION FORCE
SERIES

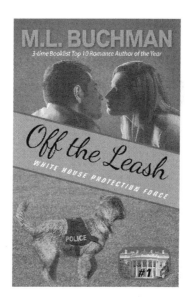

OFF THE LEASH (EXCERPT)

"You're joking."

"Nope. That's his name. And he's yours now."

Sergeant Linda Hamlin wondered quite what it would take to wipe that smile off Lieutenant Jurgen's face. A 120mm round from an M1A1 Abrams Main Battle Tank came to mind.

The kennel master of the US Secret Service's Canine Team was clearly a misogynistic jerk from the top of his polished head to the bottoms of his equally polished boots. She wondered if the shoelaces were polished as well.

Then she looked over at the poor dog sitting hopefully on the concrete kennel floor. His stall had a dog bed three times his size and a water bowl deep enough for him to bathe in. No toys, because toys always came from the handler as a reward. He offered her a sad sigh and a liquid doggy gaze. The kennel even smelled wrong, more of sanitizer than dog. The walls seemed to echo with each bark down the long line of kennels

housing the candidate hopefuls for the next addition to
the Secret Service's team.

Thor—really?—was a brindle-colored mutt, part
who-knew and part no-one-cared. He looked like a cross
between an oversized, long-haired schnauzer and a dust
mop that someone had spilled dark gray paint on. After
mixing in streaks of tawny brown, they'd left one white
paw just to make him all the more laughable.

And of course Lieutenant Jerk Jurgen would assign
Thor to the first woman on the USSS K-9 team.

Unable to resist, she leaned over far enough to scruff
the dog's ears. He was the physical opposite of the sleek
and powerful Malinois MWDs—military war dogs—that
she'd been handling for the 75th Rangers for the last five
years. They twitched with eagerness and nerves. A good
MWD was seventy pounds of pure drive—every damn
second of the day. If the mild-mannered Thor weighed
thirty pounds, she'd be surprised. And he looked like a
little girl's best friend who should have a pink bow on his
collar.

Jurgen was clearly ex-Marine and would have no
respect for the Army. Of course, having been in the
Army's Special Operations Forces, she knew better than
to respect a Marine.

"We won't let any old swabbie bother us, will we?"

Jurgen snarled—definitely Marine Corps. Swabbie
was slang for a Navy sailor and a Marine always took
offense at being lumped in with them no matter how
much they belonged. Of course the swabbies took offense
at having the Marines lumped with *them*. Too bad there
weren't any Navy around so that she could get two for the

price of one. Jurgen wouldn't be her boss, so appeasing him wasn't high on her to-do list.

At least she wouldn't need any of the protective bite gear working with Thor. With his stature, he was an explosives detection dog without also being an attack one.

"Where was he trained?" She stood back up to face the beast.

"Private outfit in Montana—some place called Henderson's Ranch. Didn't make their MWD program," his scoff said exactly what he thought the likelihood of any dog outfit in Montana being worthwhile. "They wanted us to try the little runt out."

She'd never heard of a training program in Montana. MWDs all came out of Lackland Air Force Base training. The Secret Service mostly trained their own and they all came from Vohne Liche Kennels in Indiana. Unless... Special Operations Forces dogs were trained by private contractors. She'd worked beside a Delta Force dog for a single month—he'd been incredible.

"Is he trained in English or German?" Most American MWDs were trained in German so that there was no confusion in case a command word happened to be part of a spoken sentence. It also made it harder for any random person on the battlefield to shout something that would confuse the dog.

"German according to his paperwork, but he won't listen to me much in either language."

Might as well give the diminutive Thor a few basic tests. A snap of her fingers and a slap on her thigh had the dog dropping into a smart "heel" position. No need to call out *Fuss*—*by my foot.*

"*Pass auf!*" *Guard!* She made a pistol with her thumb and forefinger and aimed it at Jurgen as she grabbed her forearm with her other hand—the military hand sign for enemy.

The little dog snarled at Jurgen sharply enough to have him backing out of the kennel. "Goddamn it!"

"*Ruhig.*" *Quiet.* Thor maintained his fierce posture but dropped the snarl.

"*Gute Hund.*" *Good dog,* Linda countered the command.

Thor looked up at her and wagged his tail happily. She tossed him a doggie treat, which he caught midair and crunched happily.

She didn't bother looking up at Jurgen as she knelt once more to check over the little dog. His scruffy fur was so soft that it tickled. Good strength in the jaw, enough to show he'd had bite training despite his size—perfect if she ever needed to take down a three-foot-tall terrorist. Legs said he was a jumper.

"Take your time, Hamlin. I've got nothing else to do with the rest of my goddamn day except babysit you and this mutt."

"Is the course set?"

"Sure. Take him out," Jurgen's snarl sounded almost as nasty as Thor's before he stalked off.

She stood and slapped a hand on her opposite shoulder.

Thor sprang aloft as if he was attached to springs and she caught him easily. He'd cleared well over double his own height. Definitely trained...and far easier to catch than seventy pounds of hyperactive Malinois.

She plopped him back down on the ground. On lead or off? She'd give him the benefit of the doubt and try off first to see what happened.

Linda zipped up her brand-new USSS jacket against the cold and led the way out of the kennel into the hard sunlight of the January morning. Snow had brushed the higher hills around the USSS James J. Rowley Training Center—which this close to Washington, DC, wasn't saying much—but was melting quickly. Scents wouldn't carry as well on the cool air, making it more of a challenge for Thor to locate the explosives. She didn't know where they were either. The course was a test for handler as well as dog.

Jurgen would be up in the observer turret looking for any excuse to mark down his newest team. Perhaps teasing him about being just a Marine hadn't been her best tactical choice. She sighed. At least she was consistent—she'd always been good at finding ways to piss people off before she could stop herself and consider the wisdom of doing so.

This test was the culmination of a crazy three months, so she'd forgive herself this time—something she also wasn't very good at.

In October she'd been out of the Army and unsure what to do next. Tucked in the packet with her DD 214 honorable discharge form had been a flyer on career opportunities with the US Secret Service dog team: *Be all your dog can be!* No one else being released from Fort

Benning that day had received any kind of a job flyer at all that she'd seen, so she kept quiet about it.

She had to pass through DC on her way back to Vermont—her parent's place. Burlington would work for, honestly, not very long at all, but she lacked anywhere else to go after a decade of service. So, she'd stopped off in DC to see what was up with that job flyer. Five interviews and three months to complete a standard six-month training course later—which was mostly a cakewalk after fighting with the US Rangers—she was on-board and this chill January day was her first chance with a dog. First chance to prove that she still had it. First chance to prove that she hadn't made a mistake in deciding that she'd seen enough bloodshed and war zones for one lifetime and leaving the Army.

The Start Here sign made it obvious where to begin, but she didn't dare hesitate to take in her surroundings past a quick glimpse. Jurgen's score would count a great deal toward where she and Thor were assigned in the future. Mostly likely on some field prep team, clearing the way for presidential visits.

As usual, hindsight informed her that harassing the lieutenant hadn't been an optimal strategy. A hindsight that had served her equally poorly with regular Army commanders before she'd finally hooked up with the Rangers—kowtowing to officers had never been one of her strengths.

Thankfully, the Special Operations Forces hadn't given a damn about anything except performance and *that* she could always deliver, since the day she'd been named the team captain for both soccer and volleyball.

She was never popular, but both teams had made all-state her last two years in school.

The canine training course at James J. Rowley was a two-acre lot. A hard-packed path of tramped-down dirt led through the brown grass. It followed a predictable pattern from the gate to a junker car, over to tool shed, then a truck, and so on into a compressed version of an intersection in a small town. Beyond it ran an urban street of gray clapboard two- and three-story buildings and an eight-story office tower, all without windows. Clearly a playground for Secret Service training teams.

Her target was the town, so she blocked the city street out of her mind. Focus on the problem: two roads, twenty storefronts, six houses, vehicles, pedestrians.

It might look normal...normalish with its missing windows and no movement. It would be anything but. Stocked with fake IEDs, a bombmaker's stash, suicide cars, weapons caches, and dozens of other traps, all waiting for her and Thor to find. He had to be sensitive to hundreds of scents and it was her job to guide him so that he didn't miss the opportunity to find and evaluate each one.

There would be easy scents, from fertilizer and diesel fuel used so destructively in the 1995 Oklahoma City bombing, to almost as obvious TNT to the very difficult to detect C-4 plastic explosive.

Mannequins on the street carried grocery bags and briefcases. Some held fresh meat, a powerful smell demanding any dog's attention, but would count as a false lead if they went for it. On the job, an explosives detection dog wasn't supposed to care about anything except explosives. Other mannequins were wrapped in suicide vests loaded with Semtex or wearing knapsacks filled with package bombs made from Russian PVV-5A.

She spotted Jurgen stepping into a glassed-in observer turret atop the corner drugstore. Someone else was already there and watching.

She looked down once more at the ridiculous little dog and could only hope for the best.

"Thor?"

He looked up at her.

She pointed to the left, away from the beaten path.

"*Such!*" Find.

Thor sniffed left, then right. Then he headed forward quickly in the direction she pointed.

———

CLIVE ANDREWS SAT IN THE SECOND-STORY WINDOW AT THE corner of Main and First, the only two streets in town. Downstairs was a drugstore all rigged to explode, except there were no triggers and there was barely enough explosive to blow up a candy box.

Not that he'd know, but that's what Lieutenant Jurgen had promised him.

It didn't really matter if it was rigged to blow for real, because when Miss Watson—never Ms. or Mrs.—asked for a "favor," you did it. At least he did. Actually, he had yet to meet anyone else who knew her. Not that he'd asked around. She wasn't the sort of person one talked about with strangers, or even close friends. He'd bet even if they did, it would be in whispers. That's just what she was like.

So he'd traveled across town from the White House and into Maryland on a cold winter's morning, barely past a sunrise that did nothing to warm the day. Now he sat in an unheated glass icebox and watched a new officer run a test course he didn't begin to understand.

———

Keep reading at fine retailers everywhere:
Off the Leash
...and don't forget that review. It really helps me out.

ABOUT THE AUTHOR

M.L. Buchman started the first of over 60 novels, 100 short stories, and a fast-growing pile of audiobooks while flying from South Korea to ride his bicycle across the Australian Outback. Part of a solo around the world trip that ultimately launched his writing career in: thrillers, military romantic suspense, contemporary romance, and SF/F.

PW says his thrillers will make "Tom Clancy fans open to a strong female lead clamor for more." His titles have been named Barnes & Noble and NPR "Top 5 of the year" and 3-time Booklist "Top 10 of the Year" as well as being a "Top 20 Modern Masterpiece" in romantic suspense.

As a 30-year project manager with a geophysics degree who has: designed and built houses, flown and jumped out of planes, and solo-sailed a 50' ketch—he is awed by what's possible. More at: www.mlbuchman.com.

Other works by M. L. Buchman: *(★ - also in audio)*

Other works by M. L. Buchman:

Contemporary Romance (cont)

Where Dreams
Where Dreams are Born
Where Dreams Reside
Where Dreams Are of Christmas
Where Dreams Unfold
Where Dreams Are Written

Science Fiction / Fantasy

Deities Anonymous
Cookbook from Hell: Reheated
Saviors 101

Single Titles
The Nara Reaction
Monk's Maze
the Me and Elsie Chronicles

Non-Fiction

Strategies for Success
Managing Your Inner Artist/Writer
Estate Planning for Authors*
Character Voice
Narrate and Record Your Own
Audiobook*

Short Story Series by M. L. Buchman:

Romantic Suspense

Delta Force
Delta Force

Firehawks
The Firehawks Lookouts
The Firehawks Hotshots
The Firebirds

The Night Stalkers
The Night Stalkers
The Night Stalkers 5E
The Night Stalkers CSAR
The Night Stalkers Wedding Stories

US Coast Guard
US Coast Guard

White House Protection Force
White House Protection Force

Contemporary Romance

Eagle Cove
Eagle Cove

Henderson's Ranch
Henderson's Ranch*

Where Dreams
Where Dreams

Thrillers

Dead Chef
Dead Chef

Science Fiction / Fantasy

Deities Anonymous
Deities Anonymous

Other
The Future Night Stalkers
Single Titles

SIGN UP FOR M. L. BUCHMAN'S NEWSLETTER TODAY

Printed in Great Britain
by Amazon